# My First COUNTING BOOK

By Lilian Moore
Pictures by Garth Williams

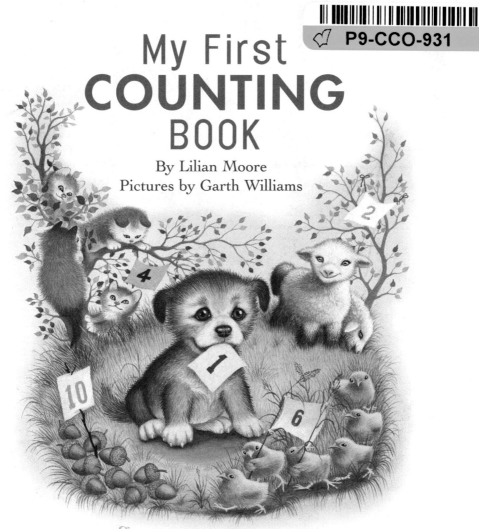

A GOLDEN BOOK • NEW YORK

Published in the United States by Golden Books, an imprint of Random House Children's Books,
a division of Random House, Inc., New York. Originally published in 1956 in slightly different
form by Simon and Schuster, Inc., and Artists and Writers Guild, Inc. GOLDEN BOOKS,
A GOLDEN BOOK, A LITTLE GOLDEN BOOK, the G colophon, and the distinctive gold spine are
registered trademarks of Random House, Inc. A Little Golden Book Classic is a trademark
of Random House, Inc.
www.goldenbooks.com
www.randomhouse.com/kids
Educators and librarians, for a variety of teaching tools, visit us at www.randomhouse.com/teachers
Library of Congress Control Number: 2007923343
ISBN: 978-0-307-02067-3
Printed in the United States of America

**1**

One little puppy,
A roly-poly puppy, alone as he can be.
"Isn't there a boy or girl
Who wants to play with me?"

Two little woolly lambs
Looking for their mother.
Two little woolly lambs,
A sister and a brother.

2

**3**

Mother Horse
And Daddy Horse
Are proud as they can be . . .

Because they have a baby horse,
And baby horse makes three.

Four furry, purry kittens
Look alike because

Each furry, purry kitten
Has four white paws.

5

Bunny finds five cabbages—
One, two, three, four, five—
Near the garden wall.
Bunny sniffs five cabbages,
And Bunny wants them all.

One, two, three,
Four, five, six.
First they were eggs . . .

Now, they are chicks!

Waddle, waddle, waddle,
The baby ducklings go,
Waddling after Mother Duck,
Seven in a row.

7

Swish, swish,
Eight fish
Swimming in the brook . . .

**8**

Swish, swish,
Wise fish,
Swimming past the hook.

High in the sky
In the shape of a "V,"
How many wild geese
Can you see?

Hurry and count them
As they fly.
You will see nine geese,
And so will I!

How many nuts did you find,
Little Squirrel,
Looking high and low?
Chitter, chatter,
What's the matter?
Don't you know?
Little Squirrel, I'll tell you, then.
Little Squirrel, you found ten.

**10**

| | |
|---|---|
| 1 | ONE |
| 2 | TWO |
| 3 | THREE |
| 4 | FOUR |
| 5 | FIVE |

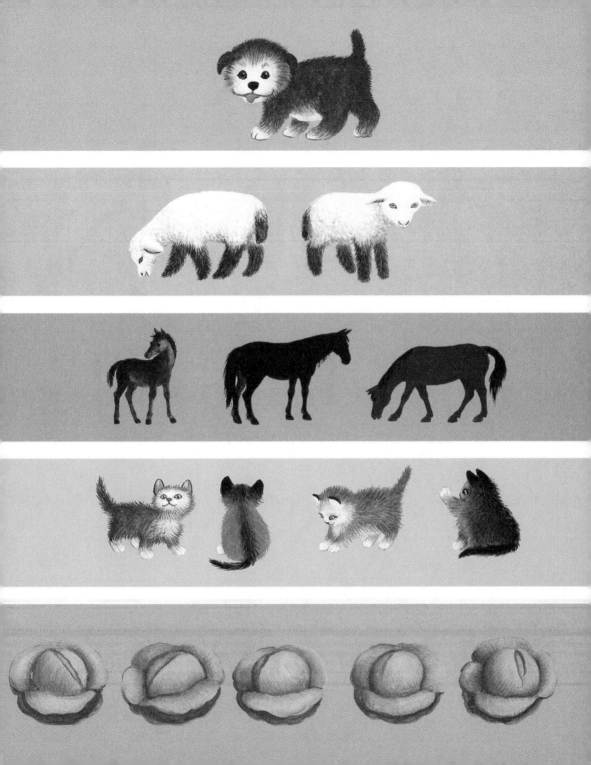

| | |
|---|---|
| 6 | SIX |
| 7 | SEVEN |
| 8 | EIGHT |
| 9 | NINE |
| 10 | TEN |

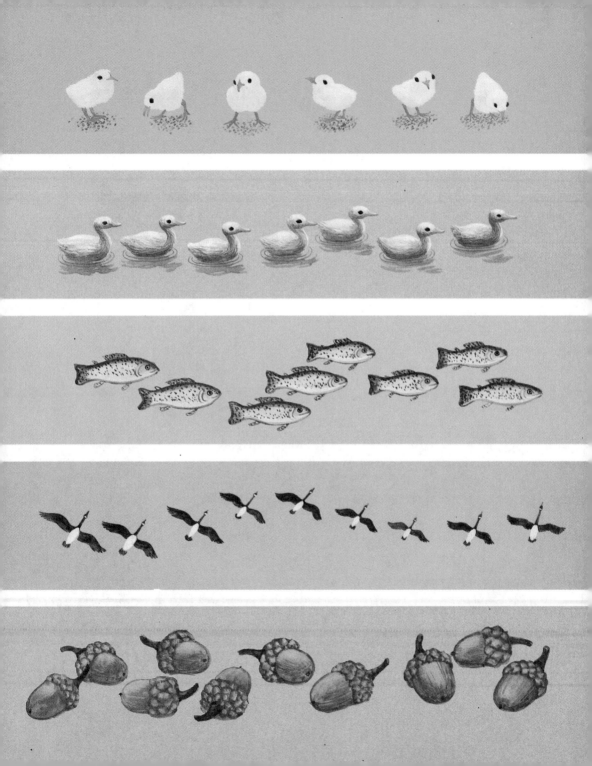